Text copyright © 2003 by Nord-Süd Verlag AG, Gossau Zürich, Switzerland.
First published in Switzerland under the title *Der kleinste Zirkus der Welt*.
English translation copyright © 2003 by North-South Books Inc., New York

First published in the United States, Great Britain, Canada, Australia, and New Zealand in
2003 by North-South Books, an imprint of Nord-Süd Verlag AG, Gossau Zürich, Switzerland.

Distributed in the United States by North-South Books Inc., New York.

Library of Congress Cataloging-in-Publication Data is available.
A CIP catalogue record for this book is available from The British Library.

ISBN 0-7358-1787-1 (trade edition)
1 3 5 7 9 HC 10 8 6 4 2
ISBN 0-7358-1788-X (library edition)
1 3 5 7 9 LE 10 8 6 4 2
Printed in Belgium

For more information about our books, and the authors and artists
who create them, visit our web site: www.northsouth.com

The Smallest Circus in the World

By Mariana Fedorova

Illustrated by Eugen Sopko

Translated by J. Alison James

North-South Books

New York * London

For years, the beloved clown Leo Mousini was the star attraction at the circus. How wonderful he was, in his bright orange jacket and black bowler hat. Every evening he performed astonishing acrobatic feats, daring balancing acts, and complicated juggling tricks. Audiences loved him—especially the children.

But as the years passed and Leo Mousini grew older, the tricks grew harder and harder to do. Standing on one arm made him dizzy. His back ached after handsprings. And balancing on his toes on the top of a ladder made the circus ring swim before his eyes.

One evening, his whole body groaned with pain. Leo Mousini had to admit it. He was too old to be a clown.

At the next performance, Leo Mousini walked quietly into the middle of the ring. "Ladies and gentlemen," he said, "I am sorry to tell you that I am leaving the circus and I will not be coming back. Even clowns grow old."

Leo Mousini took a deep bow so that nobody would see his tears. He bowed so low that his hat tumbled off his head and rolled to the edge of the ring.

Two mice were hiding there under the curtain. They wanted to be clowns themselves and every night they watched Leo Mousini's performance, trying to learn from him. And now Leo Mousini was leaving the circus! Without a second thought, the two mice hopped onto the hat and hid beneath its band. Leo Mousini didn't notice his passengers when he picked up his hat and left the ring.

He didn't notice his guests when he got home that night. He still didn't know they were there when he woke the next morning.

Leo Mousini decided to take one last walk around the circus wagons. His heart was heavy. "I'll miss my circus life very much," he said to himself. "I wonder what I'll do?"

A trumpet fanfare blasted the early morning air. Someone shouted "Long live Leo Mousini, master clown!"

The ringmaster had spread a great table full of food and prepared a wonderful farewell party. Leo put on a happy face, for that was what clowns do best. Nobody could tell how sad he was. Nobody could know how afraid he was that there was nothing left for him do with his life.

Leo Mousini trundled off pulling his little circus wagon, looking for a good place to camp for his first night on his own. That was when he finally noticed something scrambling around on his hat.

"We are Mitzi and Mack," said the mice. "We want to be clowns, just like you."

"You are awfully small," replied the old clown.

"We might be small, but we are determined," said Mack.

"Well," Leo Mousini said, "a lot can be accomplished with determination."

Over the next few weeks Leo Mousini
built miniature musical instruments, chairs, a
ladder, and other things the mice would need
for a circus performance. Then he made them
each a black felt hat.

He taught the little clowns tumbling until
their legs and backs ached. He taught them
juggling until their paws were red. But the
mice did not give up.

When Mitzi and Mack were able to balance on one hand and do back flips from the ladder, Leo Mousini said, "Get a pair of scissors. It's time to make your costumes."

Mitzi cut pieces from the cuffs of Leo's clown pants—just enough for two pairs of mouse trousers.

Mack snipped the pockets from Leo's jacket to make tiny bright orange jackets, and they clipped a bit of leather from his shoes to make two pairs of their own. With their black bowler hats, the costumes were complete.

Leo Mousini laughed to see them. "This evening we'll present our first performance in the town square," he cried.

Late that afternoon, Leo Mousini popped on his hat. Hip hop, the two little mice flipped over the rim and danced up to the crown. Leo Mousini blew a cheerful blast on his trumpet as they marched into town.

"Here comes the Mini-Mousini Circus! Come one, come all! Come see the smallest circus in the world!" cried Leo Mousini. With a great flourish, he set up his table in the town square. His bowler hat was the circus ring. Children gathered round, and then the grown-ups did, too. Everyone wanted to see the Mini-Mousini Circus.

Mitzi and Mack performed astonishing acrobatic feats, daring balancing acts, and complicated juggling routines. The audience was amazed. "Bravo!" they cried. "Three cheers for the Mini-Mousini Circus!"

When the performance was over, Leo Mousini turned to Mitzi and Mack. "You know," he said, "I thought I was finished with circus life, and I confess that made me sad. But you two have given me something wonderful to do for as long as I live." Then, blowing a fanfare on his trumpet, Leo bowed to the two little mice and said, "Leo Mousini, ringmaster for the smallest circus in the world."